CONTENTS

CHAPTER 1

The beginning of my adventures

My name is Doctor Lemuel Gulliver. I am 42 years old, and in these four decades, I have had many amazing adventures. I will tell you about some of them.

I finished medical school when I was 24. Just being a doctor was far too boring for me, so I decided to join a ship. I spent many years travelling to far off places. This allowed me to earn enough money to send back to my wife, and also gave me the opportunity to learn many kinds of languages.

I was on the ship, the Antelope, which was near the western coast of Australia when a terrible storm came upon us. The ship was thrown on sharp-edged rocks and it sank. A few of my fellow sailors and I managed to get into a boat. We rowed and rowed for as long as our arms would allow us to. Exhausted and weak, we were no match for the fast currents and strong winds. Our boat tossed about and eventually overturned.

I do not know what happened to my shipmates. I was thrown into the violent sea and could barely manage to keep afloat. Just as I was about to give in to exhaustion, my feet suddenly touched bottom. Though it was nighttime, up ahead in the distance I saw what looked like lights.

I began swimming through the water. The coast was visible but far. It took me two hours to reach a safe point. Since I had reached a carpet of soft grass, I knew the sea could no longer pose a danger. I crashed on the grass and fell into a deep, deep sleep.

CHAPTER 2

How I reached Lilliput

I must have slept for a very long time, for when I woke up, it was broad daylight. I felt quite strange and stiff. Trying to move my arms and legs, I suddenly discovered that I could not. Looking down slightly, I now noticed that my arms and legs were tied with thin, cord-like ropes and pegged to the ground. Even my chest and thighs were fixed down. My hair was separated into sections and then pinned down as well.

I was shocked! I just could not understand how this had happened. Soon I became aware of some sounds around me. Then, I felt as if something was crawling up my body. When it reached my chin, I lowered my eyes to see what it was. To my astonishment, I found myself looking at a tiny human being. He was not more than six inches tall!

About 40 others followed the first tiny man.
They were all carrying bows and arrows. One of
them climbed onto my chin and peered closely
at my face. Then he turned away and
announced in a loud voice, "Hekinah degul!"
"Hekinah degul!" repeated all his countrymen.

I had no idea what they were saying. All I wanted to do was to free myself. I tugged at the strings with all my might. Unfortunately, I only managed to free my left hand and some sections of my hair. This allowed me to turn my head to the right.

Then I tried to pick up some of the small beings with my free hand. Immediately, I was hit by a volley of arrows. While the arrows did not hurt that much, they definitely stung like a million pin-pricks. They even began pricking me in my face and poking me with their spears.

I decided to lie as still as possible, hoping they would stop attacking me. My plan worked. They left me in peace. Soon I heard some sounds similar to those made by carpenters. Turning my head, I saw about 50 carpenters setting up a platform that was about a foot and a half above the ground.

A rather important looking man and his attendants climbed onto the platform. He began making a long speech. I did not understand any of it, though I did notice that he used the word 'Lilliput' very often. I tried to speak to him in English but it was useless. Finally, I pointed to my mouth and gestured to him that I wanted food and drink. By now, I was very hungry.

The Emperor, for it was him who had been talking to me, then signalled to his people. They climbed up to my chin and filled my mouth with enormous quantities of mutton, chicken, fish and vegetables. But the tiny sizes made me feel like they were mere crumbs. Then, they brought two barrels full of some wine-like liquid. This too, they emptied into my mouth.

Then, a man, who seemed like a minister, came towards my face and spoke to me. He pointed towards the city that I could see and kept repeating, 'Mildendo'. I understood that they were planning to shift me to their capital city. I nodded in agreement. Soon, the wine made me drowsy and I fell off to sleep again.

I believe from the moment the Emperor had learnt about my arrival, he had ordered five hundred carpenters to construct a seven feet by four feet long trolley for me. This was what was used to transport me to Mildendo. To hoist me onto the trolley, they had made use of a great many pulleys.

Fifteen hundred horses (not more than four and a half inch high) and a thousand guards were required to transport me. I could not but feel deep admiration for these brilliant Lilliputians.

Once I reached the city, I found the Emperor and his Council of Ministers perched on a tower in the city wall. From this point (approximately five feet high) the Emperor pointed to what looked like the largest building in town. It was about four feet high and had an entrance, which was around two feet wide. This would allow me to enter and lie down quite comfortably, and was to be my home for the near future.

A hundred chains had been attached to one wall of this house. The other ends of the chains were now fastened on my leg with 36 locks!

After this was done, the ropes that I had been tied with were chopped off. I immediately stood up and stretched my legs by walking as far as my chains would allow me to. Seeing my full size, the Lilliputians let out cries of astonishment.

Standing also allowed me to see the city of Mildendo well. It was in the shape of a square with a high wall surrounding it. The city had two main streets at the crossing of which lay the royal palace. Three to four-storied houses were common, and well-stocked shops were a plenty.

CHAPTER 3

How the Lilliputians accepted me

The Emperor approached me on horseback.
I lay down to take a better look at him. He
seemed unafraid and proud. He was a strong,
young man and was dressed simply. Yet his
crown was radiant with jewels and left no doubt
about his status. He spoke to me and then
ordered his various advisors to speak to me as
well. I replied in many languages but none of
them could understand anything that I said.

I realised that I would have to learn their language fast. I was left under the watchful eyes of the royal guards. I was actually quite glad to have the guards around. There were a number of people who were there to see me. They made me uneasy. Some troublemakers looked determined to cause me discomfort.

Soon enough, one of them shot an arrow in my direction that almost hit my eye.

How the Lilliputians accepted me

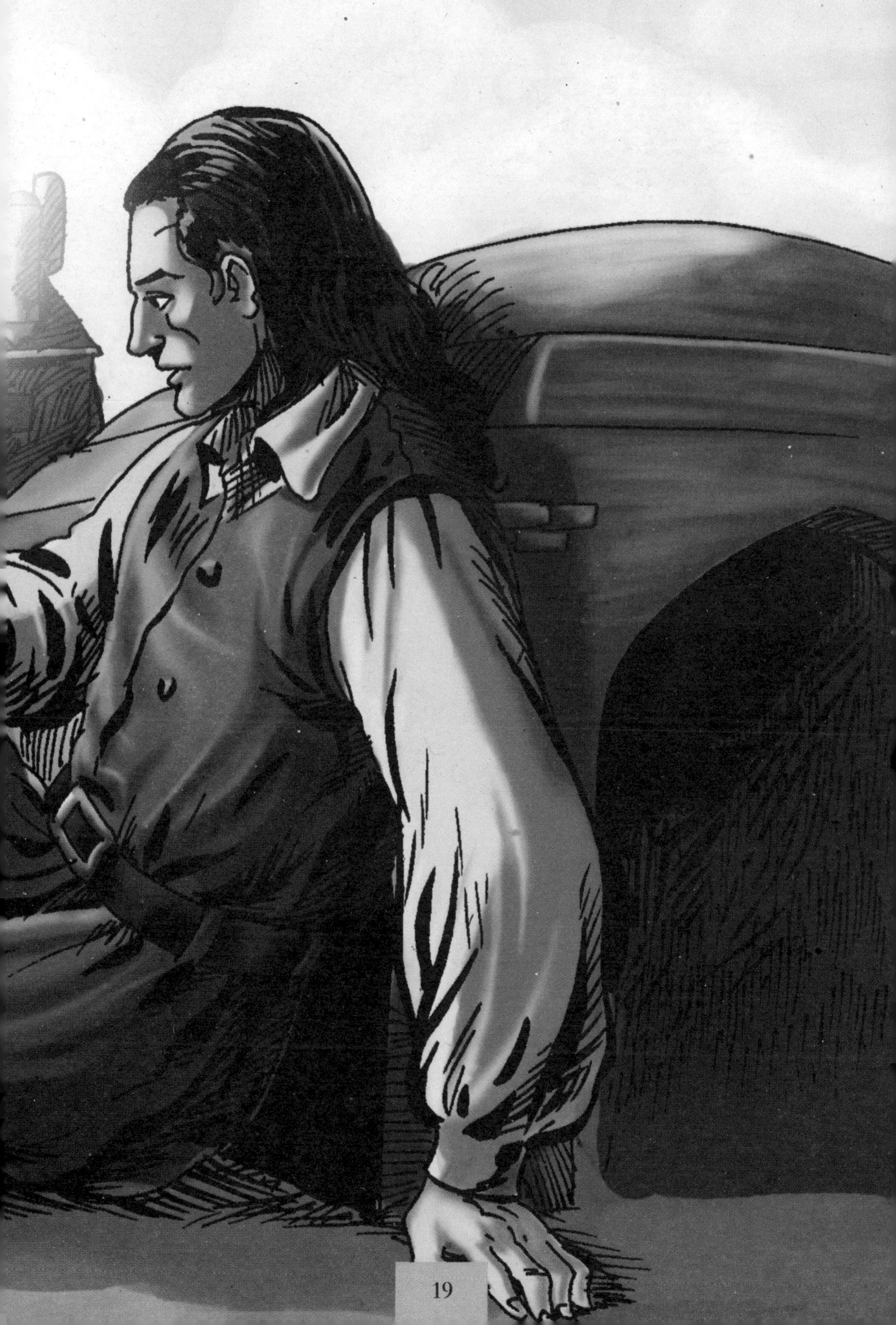

The guards immediately gathered the offenders and pushed them towards me. I picked them up and pretended that I was going to swallow them alive. They were terrified and kicked their arms and legs wildly to get loose.

They had learnt their lesson and I had also managed to communicate to everybody else that I did not wish to be ill-treated. Having accomplished my mission, I set them down gently. While they ran as fast as their legs could carry them, I noticed that the onlookers were happy with my reaction.

Meanwhile, the Emperor continued to be hospitable. After a few nights, I found that a mattress had been especially made for me. It was made from five hundred Lilliputian mattresses kept lengthwise, and one hundred and fifty mattresses kept in four layers, to create a comfortable bed for me.

While I was settling into my new home, the Emperor and his Council of Ministers were discussing my future. I had made a new friend in court who was kind enough to give me information regarding this matter.

Some of the ministers were concerned that I would free myself from the chains and walk all over their city, destroying expensive buildings and people. Others were worried that my stay and food bills would be very expensive.

In the midst of this conversation, a few noblemen walked in and told the Emperor of my kindness in dealing with the troublemakers. This impressed the Emperor so much that he then ordered the neighbouring villages to provide food for me everyday. The Emperor said that he would pay for this from his personal wealth.

The Emperor also hired six hundred servants and engaged six of the country's greatest scholars to teach me the Lilliputian language. I took these classes very seriously, and as soon as I was able to, I went to His Majesty and said, "Please set me free!"

The Emperor asked me to be patient and then informed me about a law in Lilliput. Every visitor had to be searched for weapons. I lifted the officers responsible for the job, onto my various pockets. I had my glasses, compass and telescope hidden in one inner pocket. I did not disclose that pocket.

The officers made a detailed list of my belongings. The list included items that were on me, like my diary, my comb, my snuffbox, pistol, two knives (one that I used as a razor, and the other as a penknife), some gold coins and my watch. I was also wearing a belt with a pouch of gunpowder and some bullets. They asked me to unsheathe my sword and place it on the ground. I did so.

Next, they asked me to demonstrate how my pistol worked. Though I warned them regarding the noise it would create, the impact it had on them was astonishing. The force of the explosion threw most of them off the floor, and had them falling flat on their faces.

CHAPTER 4

How the Lilliputians set me free

Very soon the Lilliputians lost all fear of me. They even allowed their children to play on me or hide in my hair. I encouraged this hoping it would secure a faster release for me.

To entertain me and keep me occupied, His Majesty would often organise shows of skill and artistry for me. My favourite show was the one in which ropewalkers balanced themselves on a thin white thread about two feet off the ground. But I was shocked when I learnt that these ropewalkers were actually competing for top government posts!

Flimnap, the Finance Minister was given his post because he jumped an inch higher than everybody else on the rope. The only person who could come close to his record was Reldresal, the Emperor's Private Secretary, who had become a good friend of mine.

How the Lilliputians set me free

As time went by, I would keep requesting and pleading with His Majesty to set me free. His whole council was in my favour except the High Admiral, Skyresh Bolgolam. Finally, he too agreed to my release but only if I would sign and obey some conditions.

When the final list of conditions was drawn up, it included the following rules:

- I could not leave Lilliput without the Emperor's permission.
- I could not enter the city without giving two hours notice.
- I had to be careful while walking, so as not to destroy the people or their belongings.
- I could not pick up anyone without his or her consent.
- I would act as the Emperor's messenger whenever he would require me to.
- I would help in the war against Blefuscu, the sworn enemy of Lilliput.
- I would also be required to help lift large boulders and measure the circumference of the land.

Even though I did not want to do many of the things that were put down, I knew I did not have a choice. I was still dependant on these people for food, water, shelter, clothing and everything else.

As soon as I had agreed to all the conditions, my chains were unlocked and I was free to roam around, at last!

CHAPTER 5

My stay as a free man

My first request to the Emperor was to be allowed to see the city of Mildendo. I was granted permission, and people were informed well in advance, so that they did not get hurt, even accidentally. I strolled along the city's main streets, and came to the central square where the royal palace was situated. I proceeded to the palace and peeped in.

I saw the most grand and beautiful apartments that I had ever laid my eyes on. The Empress and her companions were watching over the young princes and princesses as they played. This was very unusual because all other Lilliputian children had to stay away from home in nurseries. They were allowed to go home only twice a year and that too for half an hour.

When the Empress saw me, she came out to her balcony, and held out her hand for me to kiss it. I was overjoyed!

The Emperor granted me permission to cut down the largest trees in the royal gardens to make myself a table and a chair. Two hundred tailors were put to work to sew a new set of clothes for me. Since they had created it out of different bales of cloth, my suit began looking like a patchwork quilt.

Now that I had my own table, servants and some new clothes, I decided it was time for me to return the hospitality I was enjoying. I invited the Emperor, Empress along with the Finance Minister, Flimnap, for dinner to my house.

When Flimnap thought I was not listening, I saw him telling His Majesty that I should be sent away as I had already used up more than a million gold coins.

The Finance Minister was also very jealous of me since his wife liked to spend a lot of time in my company!

She would come with her children or with her sister and ask me endless questions about the English ladies. Flimnap did not like this and became very annoyed with me. He began advising the Emperor against me.

One day, I saw my friend Reldresal coming to my house in the morning. He had come to warn me about a threat Lilliput was facing. There appeared to be a strong possibility of a war as Blefuscu was planning to attack Lilliput.

The enmity between the two countries began in the days of the current Emperor's grandfather. It was now known that the Blefuscudians had rebuilt their shipping fleet and were planning to attack, using their great naval might.

Reldresal asked me to help the Emperor to defend his country against the Blefuscudians. I agreed and thought it was a genuine way to show my appreciation for all that he had done for me.

CHAPTER 6

The war and peace with Blefuscu

Having promised to help the Emperor, I began
to stay away from the coastline, so that the
Blefuscudians couldn't see me. I also began to
find out more about their fleet and where it was
stationed. Having studied the fleet at length
through my telescope, I realised there were
about 50 ships. I ordered iron hooks and
attached them to strong cords. I found out that
the deepest part of the channel was about six
feet deep.

I waited for the perfect moment and then swam to the Blefuscudian coast. Thousands of soldiers just jumped from the ships and ran away when they saw me approaching. I was pelted with arrows but was lucky to stay unhurt. Apart from that, it was quite easy for me to hook the ships, cut their anchors and drag them to the Lilliputian coast.

The Emperor was so delighted with my accomplishment that he awarded me with the title of Nardac, the highest honour in the land! However, I was disturbed by what he asked me to do next. He now wanted me to get the civilian ships as well, and make the people his slaves. This I could not do, as it seemed wrong to me.

After a few weeks, six ambassadors arrived from Blefuscu to ask for peace. They thanked me for convincing the Emperor not to attack them again. Then they invited me to visit their country. I asked the Emperor for permission. Though it was given, his manner was very cold and distant. I knew my enemies at court had managed to turn the Emperor against me.

Soon after this incident, I was woken up in the middle of the night. A hundred people were pounding on my door. I was asked to help as the royal apartments had caught fire.

I knew that the Lilliputian buckets would not hold enough water to douse the fire. Thinking quickly, I ran towards the sea and filled my mouth with water. I ran back to the palace and spit the water on it which put out the flames. I was happy to have saved the palace from being destroyed by the fire.

However, I soon learnt that the Empress was not happy but furious with me. Nobody was allowed to spit near the palace, and by pouring a mouthful of water on the palace itself, I had shown great disrespect. The Empress was so disgusted that she had moved out of her apartment. I suddenly became very unpopular. Skyresh Bolgolam and Flimnap had also convinced the Emperor that I was a threat to the kingdom.

As a punishment, either my eyes were to be blinded or I was to be slowly starved to death. I decided to leave for Blefuscu immediately.

CHAPTER 7

My stay at Blefuscu

The Blefuscudians did not seem to be afraid of me at all. I was very thankful to be away from Lilliput and did not say anything about my troubles there.

After about three days, as I walked along the coast, I happened to spot an upturned boat. The best part was that the boat was my size, and not like the miniature ones in this land.

My stay at Blefuscu

I ran back to meet the King. "Your Majesty, may I borrow 20 of your tallest ships and three thousand seamen?" I was granted permission for all that I asked. With the help of the ships and the men, I managed to set the boat upright.

The King was a wise and calm man and I was very grateful to him as he happily gave me the permission to leave, and also promised all help.

It took me a month to organise sails, paddles and provisions. I also took along on the boat, six cows, two bulls, and many ewes and rams.

The King gave me a life-size painting of himself, and 50 tiny pouches of gold coins as a farewell gift.

On September 24, 1701, I set sail from the coast of Blefuscu at six in the morning. The next day, I spied to my delight, a British ship! I managed to climb aboard with all my belongings.

At first, the Captain did not believe the stories of my adventures. As proof, I showed him the tiny animals and the King's painting.

"You are telling us the truth. You are not mad!" said the Captain in astonishment.

When we docked in England, I gave him a cow and a pregnant sheep to show my appreciation. I then met my family–after three years. I stayed at home for a few months. But soon, I became restless and set out for another odyssey. This time, I was on a ship going to India.

CHAPTER **8**

My adventures on Adventurer

I set off on my next voyage on a ship, 'Adventurer', which was on its way to the Cape of Good Hope.

After many days of calm weather, we were suddenly hit by terrible storms called the monsoons. There was nothing to do but to take the sail down and just be tossed around on the violent sea. Soon, our water supply began to lessen.

About this time, we came upon a huge island. 12 of us got into a boat and headed towards the island to find some fresh water. On the island, all of us ventured off in different directions. After sometime, when I returned, I saw my fellow crewmen rowing away furiously without me.

It took me a minute to see why. An enormous giant like man was running after them in the water. The giant was almost 60 feet tall! Seeing the giant, I ran for my life! I hid behind some trees on top of a hill and peered out to examine the island I was on. I was surrounded by rows of corn and barley about 20 to 30 feet high! Stalks of corn towered 40 feet above my head.

Suddenly, I saw another giant like the one I had seen near the boat. He had a reaping hook in his hand and he began to chop off the stalks of the corn with a loud swishing sound.

CHAPTER 9

My stay with giants

I was about to be stamped to death when I began shouting with all my might, "STOP! PLEASE LOOK DOWN!"

The giant heard me and looked around to see who was speaking. He almost missed me but I shouted again, "HERE! I AM HERE!" The giant finally saw me and picked me up.

At first, he thought I was an insect. Seeing that I could walk on my two feet, and from my various attempts to speak to him, he realised that I was a man. He wrapped me carefully in a handkerchief and took me home.

"Look dear! See what I have got here," he told his wife, as he set me on 30 feet high dining table. His wife and two children were delighted to see me. His wife gave me a small portion of meat to eat along with them. As I ate, the whole family watched in wonder!

The farmer's nine-year-old daughter became my best friend. She took a great liking for me and began to take very good care of me. She used her doll's clothes and furniture to provide me with a clean and safe environment. At night, she hung the bed from a hook to protect me from rats. She was a very responsible little girl. I called her my 'Glumdalclitch' or 'little nurse'. She in turn called me 'Grildrig' or 'dwarf' or 'pixie'.

She also became my teacher and started to teach me their language. She told me the name of her country. It was called Brobdingnag.

Her father, however, had seen in me a money-making opportunity. He had decided to take money from the people who would come to see me.

He built a small travelling box for me in which Glumdalclitch kept her doll's quilt, so that I could be protected against too many jerks.

We travelled from one town to another. At different places, we would stop at inns. My master would announce loudly, "I am displaying an amazing creature that looks like a splacknuck. Yet, he is human. He can talk and perform many entertaining tricks!"

I would then be walking, talking and entertaining the people, hour after hour, day after day. Often, my body and throat ached from exhaustion. Even though my little nurse was always trying to protect me and tried to provide me rest, her father was ruthless. He had now become very greedy. He did not allow me to rest even when we were at home.

I became very weak. My health really suffered and I became a skeleton. The greedy farmer realised that if he drove me like this, I would not live long. He decided to take me to the capital city. There too, he made me perform for 10 hours in a day. Glumdalclitch begged of her father to spare me but he had been blinded with wealth. In the capital, the Queen heard about me and asked the farmer to present me in the court.

How I was sold

After I had done my usual tricks, the Queen was quite taken by me. She asked me many questions about my country, the people, the culture and many other issues. She seemed very happy with my answers and suddenly asked me, "Would you like to stay here?" "If my master allows," I replied graciously, though I did not feel very grateful to the farmer. "Tell me farmer, will you sell me this slave?" asked the Queen. "Only for a good price Your Majesty! You can have him for a thousand pieces of gold," said the farmer slyly. He thought it was a great deal since I would die soon in any case.

The Queen agreed and paid the price. "I request you to allow Glumdalclitch, my teacher and friend, to be allowed to visit me, Your Majesty," I pleaded with the Queen.
The Queen did not see that to be a problem if her father agreed.

The farmer saw this as a great chance to have his daughter be a part of the royal court. He readily agreed to this arrangement.

My life at court had begun. The Queen asked her carpenters to make a 12 feet by 12 feet box for me, which was to be my bedroom. The walls of the room were quilted and beautifully decorated. The furniture was fixed to the floor and the room had handles for travelling purposes.

The Queen grew so fond of me that she would not eat without placing me before her. She would personally serve me tiny bits of her food.

Every Wednesday, the national rest day, I would have dinner with the King. He and I would discuss, at length, politics and government of various countries. I really looked forward to these conversations with him.

However, all this favour from the royal couple did not go down well with some people.

The Queen's favourite dwarf was especially annoyed and very jealous of my popularity with the Queen.

One day, he pushed me into the hollow of a bone. When the Queen learnt about it she wanted to punish him severely. I pleaded on his behalf and asked her to forgive him. But the wicked creature dropped me into an enormous bowl of cream next. I would have drowned in it, had Glumdalclitch not seen me and rushed over to fish me out.

This time when the Queen had him whipped and sent away, I did not protest. I was relieved that he would no longer be around.

CHAPTER 11

How I entertained the queen

Lorbrulgrud, the capital of Brobdingnag, was a beautiful city. I got a chance to explore it when my nurse took me out in her coach to visit various parts of the city. On these occasions, she would place me in my room-cum-travel box, and allow me to talk and meet with people.

The Queen too quite enjoyed interacting with me. She especially loved to hear about my adventures at sea. One day she asked me, "Would you like to do some sailing? I am sure you miss that."

How I entertained the queen

" I would love to Your Majesty, but I do not have any vessel of my size," I replied. "If you design one, I could have it made for you. I could also provide you with a place to use it," said the Queen.

I set about designing a boat that would be appropriate for eight people like me. When it was completed, the Queen asked her people to build a trough, three hundred feet long, fifty feet wide and eight feet deep. This was filled with water, and in it my boat was set adrift.

The Queen and her friends often sat around the trough and watched me sail my boat. They helped to create wind by using their fans or asking the servants to blow on my sails. I enjoyed this activity very much.

CHAPTER 12

How an eagle saved me

Many months went by. I had lived in
Brobdingnag for two years. Everyday I dreamt of
escaping but it seemed impossible. There were
no ships to take me back home.

One summer, Glumdalclitch and I were invited
by the King and Queen to join them at their
summer palace on the beach. The journey to the
coast was a very long one and I was quite weak
when we reached.

This time, since Glumdalclitch had high fever and had to be in bed, I was put in the care of a pageboy. He carried my room-box and took me for a stroll on the beach. I fell asleep on my bed and the pageboy must have got bored and strolled off.

Suddenly, I was woken up by a jolt and the feeling that I was being lifted high above the ground. Scared, I looked out of my window.

I was horrified to see that an eagle had the handle of my box in his mouth and we were high up in the sky!

I had given up hope of being alive when I heard the sound of gunfire. One of the shots must have hit the bird because the flapping of the wings stopped immediately and my box came crashing down at an amazing speed.

Luckily, my fall was broken by water since the box fell into the sea. I was being tossed around in the sea with no hope of ever being rescued.

CHAPTER 13

How I reached home again

I must have fallen into a tired sleep for when I woke up, I heard a man's voice say distinctly, "If there is anyone inside this box speak up now!"

I was overjoyed because the language they spoke in was English! I immediate stuck my hand with my handkerchief out of the skylight and shouted, "My name is Dr Lemuel Gulliver. I have had great misfortune and would appreciate your help!"

"All right then. We will send a carpenter to create an opening for you," replied the voice.

"That won't be necessary, just ask someone to put his finger through the top hook and the roof will open," said I.

"Are you mad? How on Earth will one man lift a little house?" said the voice.

I had not realised that I was amongst my own people. There were no more giants and I was back in my own country. The captain of the ship was very understanding. Even though at first he did not believe my adventures, once I showed him some proof (like the Queen's ring or the comb I had made from her cut nail) he began to trust me. The crew of the ship took good care of me and enjoyed listening to all my tales.

As soon as I reached London, I rushed home, after thanking the Captain and his men many times. My wife and children were very happy to see me but not as happy as I was to see them. I did not want to go on another voyage ever again or so I thought…but that is another story!